The Wandering Schoolgirl

Written and Illustrated
By

Gary L. Gallegos
and
Louis C. Gallegos

ICECAT BOOKS

The Wandering Schoolgirl

BOOK 01

Written and Illustrated by
Gary L. Gallegos and Louis C. Gallegos

ISBN 0-9764308-0-0

3|07

First Printing, January 2005

Published by Icecat Books

WWW.ICECATBOOKS.COM

Printed in the United States of America

...

"Am I dreaming?"

"Calm down"

"I'll get up and nothing will be..."

"...there."

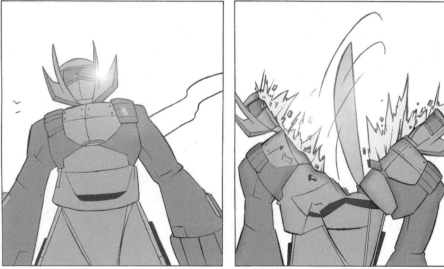

Princess Yuka's castle.
(The back entrance)

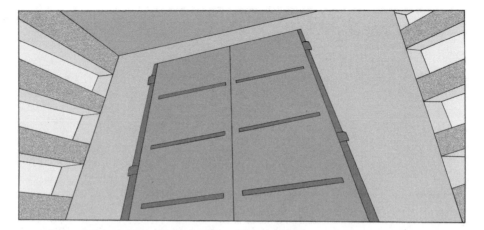

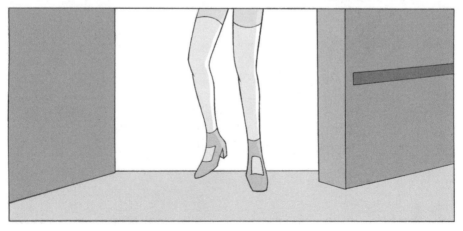

Princess Yuka.

Hanako, the leader of the coslayers, has arrived.

Entering Chibi Village.

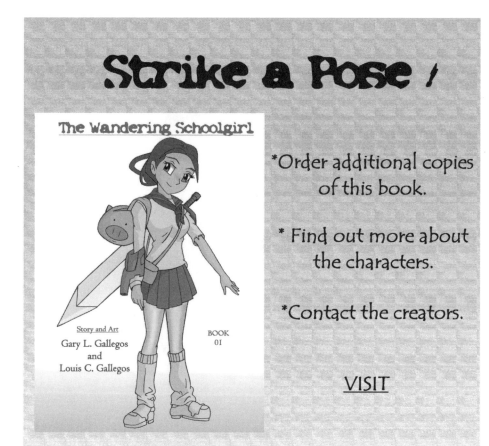